A Friend for
Henry

by Jenn Bailey
illustrated by Mika Song

chronicle books · san francisco

In Classroom Six, second left down the hall,
Henry was looking for a friend.

It couldn't be Gilly, who circled her fishbowl. *She's quiet*, thought Henry. *But she can't play on the swings.*

It couldn't be Mrs. Magoon, who knew about hugs. *She shares*, thought Henry. *But she has to.*

Could it be someone else in Classroom Six?

In Art Class, Vivianne shared Henry's double easel.

Vivianne was a kaleidoscope, a tangle of colors.
She had ribbons and clackety shoes. She knew every
pony song. Her fingernails were painted like rainbows.

"When I get paint on my fingers," Henry said,
"I wash it off."

Vivianne waved her hands *too close* to Henry's face.
"My mommy painted them. Aren't they pretty?"

"Painting on people is Against the Rules,"
said Henry. "Did your mommy get in trouble?"

"No."

Henry lowered his voice. "Did you get angry?"

"Why should I?"

But Vivianne was very angry later.
"He ruined them!"

"She likes rainbows," Henry explained.
And he thought, *a friend would say
thank you*.

Reading Time was Henry's favorite.
My friend will like it, too.

It was Henry's turn to put out the carpet squares.
He tucked the blue ones next to the brown ones.
Green in the very middle. All the edges met and
the corners fit perfectly.

"Reading Time!" shouted Samuel. "My favorite!"

Samuel was a thunderstorm, booming and crashing. He was kind of scary if you didn't have your blanket. He could pick up crayons with his toes and do proper somersaults.

Henry stepped in front of Samuel. "Somersaults are hard."

Samuel dodged past. "I want a green one!"

"Wait." Henry's throat felt tight. "They're perfect."

"Mine's a magic carpet from a genie's lamp,"
said Samuel.

"It's not!" Henry's face was hot. "It's from Rug World.
There's the sticker."

"Up, up, and away, Magic Carpet!"

Booming and crashing. Henry's fingers curled closed.

A friend listens!

"Henry." Mrs. Magoon knelt in front of him.
"Sit with me, please."

Henry did. But he couldn't see the pictures.
And his carpet square was brown.

During Snack Time, Jayden took
three crackers instead of two.

At Recess, Riley dug up worms and
let them use the swings.

At Free Time, Henry's hope for a friend felt small. He watched the sunlight play along Gilly's scales. He could watch Gilly for a long time.

Katie watched, too.

Katie smelled like strawberry milk.

She read storybooks all by herself.

She slid down the Big Slide. Sometimes backwards.

"The Big Slide is too big," said Henry.

Gilly floated past.

"She's shimmery," said Katie.

"But she doesn't blink," said Henry.

"What does she do?"

She burps pebbles, Henry thought. *And breathes underwater.
And turns sunshine into colors.*

Henry hunched into his sweatshirt. "Fish things."

Katie bent to have a closer look. "I like her."

Henry tried not to blink. "Want to play blocks?"

"Sure."

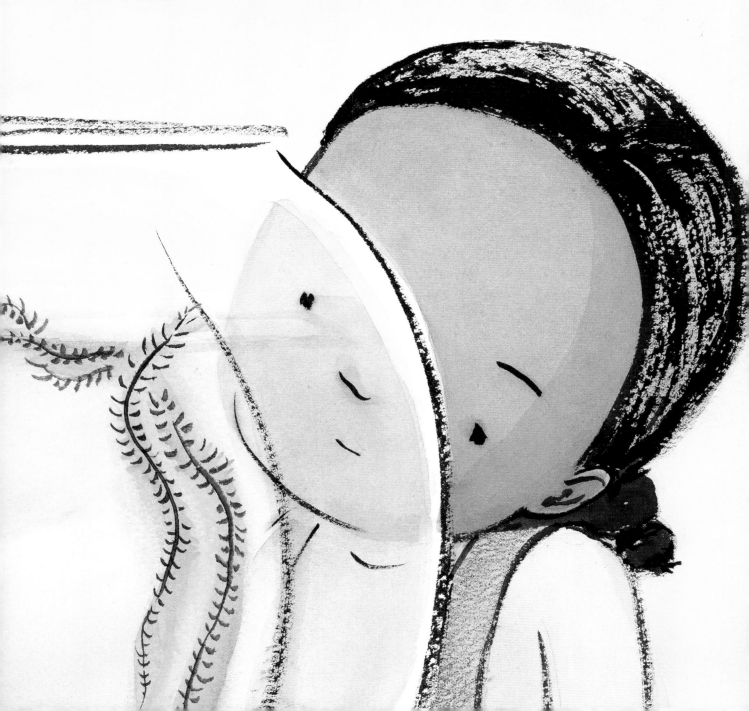

"I don't like triangles," said Henry.

"I don't like broccoli," said Katie.

Together they built a tower.

It had rectangles, cylinders, and squares.

But no triangles. Or broccoli.

"It's perfect," said Henry.

"Thank you," said Katie.

The next day, they played on the swings,
and Katie went down the Big Slide.

Henry waited at the bottom for his friend.

To Cameron, Harris, and Kellen, each
Henry in his own way.

And to K, H, and L, your patience abounds.
—J. B.

To Erica.
—M. S.

Text copyright © 2019 by Jenn Bailey.
Illustrations copyright © 2019 by Mika Song.

Library of Congress Cataloging-in-Publication Data available.

ISBN 978-1-4521-6791-6

Manufactured in China.

Design by Amelia Mack.
Typeset in Iowan Old Style.
The illustrations in this book were rendered in ink
and watercolor.

10 9 8 7 6 5 4 3

Chronicle Books LLC
680 Second Street
San Francisco, California 94107
www.chroniclekids.com